This book belongs to

_____

_____

_____

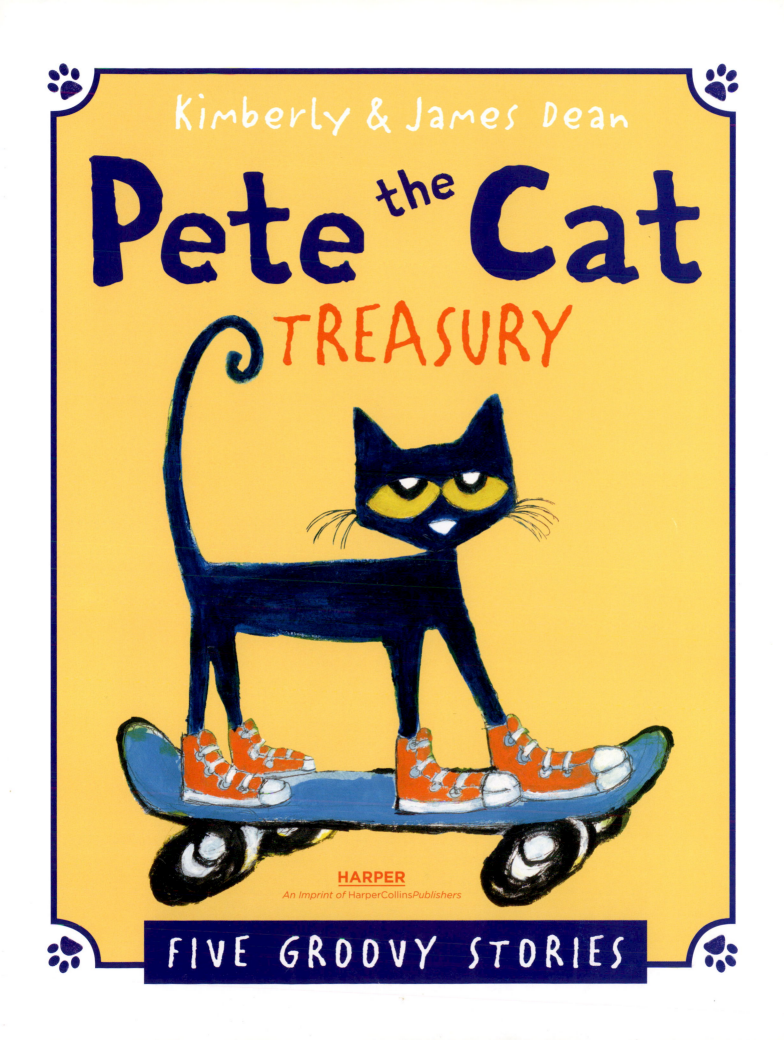

ISBN 978-0-06-274036-6

17  18  19  20  21   SCP   10  9  8  7  6  5  4  3  2  1

❖

First Edition

# Table of Contents

Page 11

Five Little Ducks

Page 45

Go, Pete, Go!

Page 73

Pete the Cat and the New Guy

Page 111

Robo-Pete

Page 137

Construction Destruction

# Who is Pete the Cat?

Everybody knows Pete: the cool, groovin' cat who rides a skateboard and rocks along with his friends. But did you know that Pete was actually a real cat?

James Dean first saw the scrawny black kitten at an animal shelter in 1999. The kitten was reaching his paw out of a cage, and James thought he was looking for a friend. James figured, *hey, why not?* That day, James took the scruffy kitten home and named him Pete.

When Pete was a kitten he loved sitting on James's lap. As James painted in his kitchen, little Pete would always be by his side. He had never spent so much time with a kitten. One day, a friend suggested to James that he draw Pete. It didn't cross his mind to draw cats—he loved drawing landscapes and old cars.

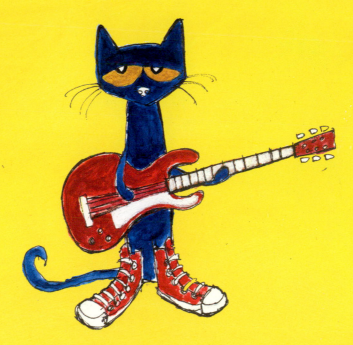

Then one day, Pete stopped his normal running around and sat still. Before James could take his photo, Pete was running around again. James usually worked from photographs and had to make a sketch of Pete from memory. When he sat down on his couch to draw Pete, he decided blue was the right color for his special cat. It was just a simple painting of a blue cat surrounded by white space.

Pete became his muse, and the rest is history. Pete the Cat has inspired James more than he'd ever imagined. Pete's adventures fill the days, weeks, and years with happiness.

**"If music be the food of love, play on!"**

—WILLIAM SHAKESPEARE

# Pete the Cat
## Five Little Ducks

F ive little ducks went out to play,
With one cool cat leading the way.

Pete the Cat said, "Let's splash and swim!"

But only four little ducks jumped in.

Four little ducks went out to play,
With one cool cat leading the way.

Pete the Cat said, "Let's jump and hop!"

But only three little ducks popped up.

Three little ducks went out to play,
With one cool cat leading the way.

Pete the Cat said, "Let's try the swings."

But only two little ducks flapped their wings.

Two little ducks went out to play,
With one cool cat leading the way.

Pete the Cat said, "Let's run inside."

But only one little duck came by.

One little duck was there to play,
With one cool cat this rainy day.

Pete the Cat said, "It's me and you!"

But that little duck left, too.

Sad Pete the Cat went out to play,
But all of the ducks had gone away.

Pete the Cat said, "Hey, what was that?"

36

And the five little ducks came running back!

Five little ducks all yelled, "Hooray!"
They made Pete a treat that day.

Pete the Cat said, "Let's all have fun."

And they played until the day was done!

The End

**"You miss 100 percent of the shots you don't take."**

—WAYNE GRETZKY

# Pete the Cat
## Go, Pete, Go!

It's a beautiful day, and Pete the Cat has decided to take his bike for a ride. Nothing makes Pete happier than feeling the sun on his fur and the breeze on his face.

Turtle has a new race car. "Who wants to have a race?" he says.

Vroom! Vroom!

"Not me," says Grumpy Toad.
"My motorcycle has a flat tire."

"Not me," says Emma.
"My car is too old and slow."

"Not me," says Callie.
"My bus is a work of art.
It's not meant for racing."

"I'll race you," says Pete, knowing how much
Turtle likes to race.
"But your bike has no motor," says Turtle.
"My race car is super quick. I'll win for sure."

"That's okay," says Pete. "I just want to
try my best and have fun."

Everyone is excited for the big race.

"On your mark. Get set. Go!" Callie shouts.

Turtle steps on the gas pedal and—vroom!—zooms away.

Pete waves good-bye
and then pedals off.

Pete sees Turtle up ahead. Turtle
slows down to let Pete catch up.

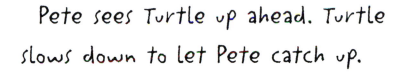

"Check this out!"
shouts Turtle. He presses a button and . . .

. . . Fins appear!

Now Turtle's race car goes even faster.

Vrrroom! Vrrroom!

Pete's bike doesn't have fins, but he does have a basket.

He stops and takes out a tasty red apple.
Nothing is better than a tasty red apple on a
beautiful day.

Turtle sees that Pete is WAY behind. He spies a
diner up ahead. "Might as well grab a bite to eat,"
Turtle says as he pulls into a parking spot.

"Yum!" says Turtle, eating a grilled-cheese sandwich. He is in no rush. He is sure he will win the race.

"Dessert?" the waitress asks. "Don't mind if I do," Turtle says.

While Turtle finishes his lunch, Pete continues pedaling. The sun is high and the breeze is blowing. It's a beautiful day for a race.

Pete sees Turtle leaving the diner. Pete waves hello, but Turtle doesn't wave back. Turtle just jumps in his car and peels off.

"I guess he didn't see me." Pete shrugs.

But Turtle did see Pete. He knows that
Pete isn't going to give up easily.

SUPER TIRES

1

So Turtle presses a button and his
tires inflate into mag wheels that
let him swerve around the curves
at top speed!

Vrrr-vrrr-vrrrooooom!

Pete passes a rosebush as he goes around
a curve. Pete knows he should keep racing,
but he can't resist.

The roses are just so beautiful. . . .
He has to stop to smell them.

Turtle sees that he has a HUGE
lead. He knows he's going to win.

LEMONADE

He stops for a nice,
cold glass of lemonade, and that's when
he sees the hammock hanging between
two trees. He's exhausted from racing so fast.
He figures a quick nap will help him in the home stretch.

Pete pedals past and sees Turtle sleeping. That's cool, Pete thinks as he rides by as quietly as he can. "Turtle must really be tired. I'm glad he's getting some rest."

Grumpy Toad finds Turtle fast asleep!

"Wake up, Turtle," says Grumpy Toad. "If you don't get back in the race, Pete is going to win."

"That's impossible," says Turtle,
thinking it must be a joke.
But it's no joke!

Turtle presses a button and rocket boosters appear, making him go super-duper fast.

Vrrrrrrooooooooooooom!

But by the time
Turtle nears the finish line . . .

# FINISH

. . . Pete has already won the race!

"How did you do it?" Turtle asks.

"Slow and steady," says Pete. "Maybe next time instead of racing, we can ride together."

"Great idea," says Turtle.

What a great race! What a great day!

# The End

**"**A man who carries a cat by the tail learns something he can learn in no other way.**"**

—MARK TWAIN

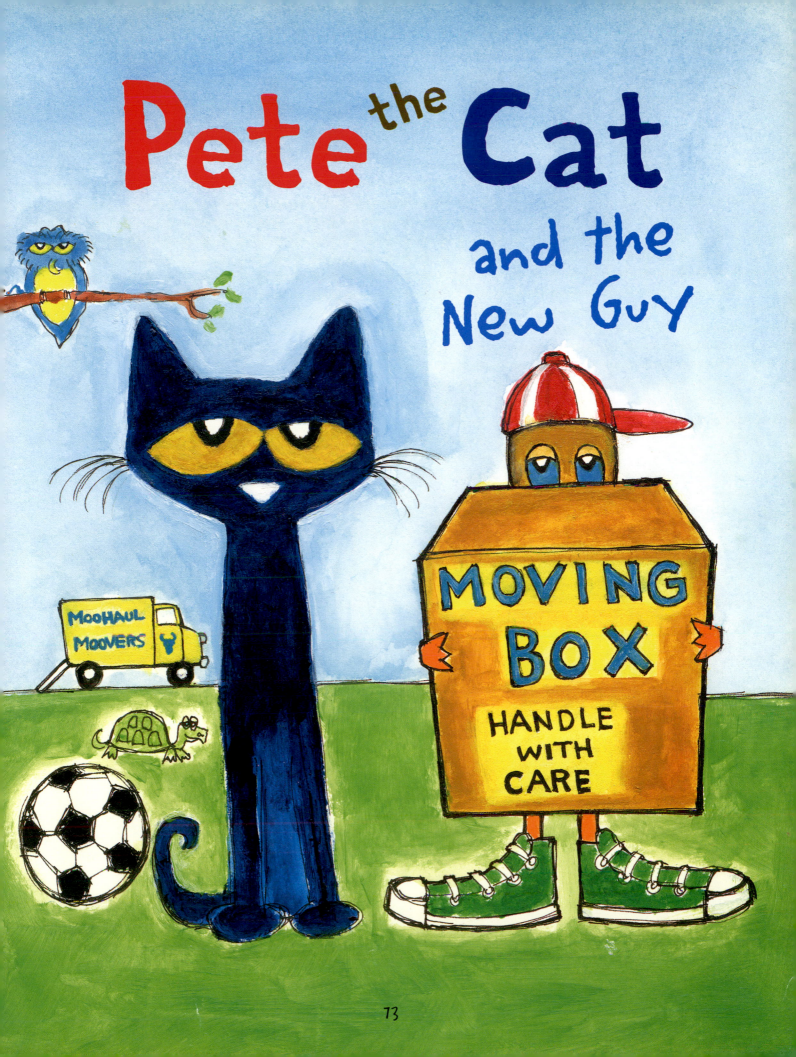

It was Sunday, and Pete's friends had come to play!
They were rocking to a new song when . . .

BEEP BEEP BEEP

There was a noise coming
from across the street!

Wise Old Owl had a view from his tree.
Pete said, "Hey, Owl! What do you see?"
Owl said, "All I see are green shoes and a red hat."
Pete answered, "Sounds like my kind of cat!"

Pete could not imagine who this new guy could be.
"I really hope it's a new friend for me."

On Monday . . .
Pete wanted to say hi, but
he was feeling kind of shy,

so he just rode by and
by and by and by—

until finally Pete got to meet the new guy.

Pete said, "I've never met anyone quite like you!
You seem like a duck, and like a beaver too!"
The new guy said to Pete, "Hi, my name is Gus.
Glad to meet you. I'm a platypus."

Pete said, "You're not like me, and I am not like you, but I think being different is really very cool."

On Tuesday . . .

Pete and Gus took a walk down the street.

They came to Squirrel, who was playing in a tree.

"Hi, Gus," said Squirrel. "Climbing is easy. Try and see."

Gus gave the tree a try, but the branch was
way too high.

"I wish I could climb like you, but climbing is
something I just can't do."

Pete said, "Don't be sad, don't be blue. There is something everyone can do!"

On Wednesday . . .

Pete and Gus took a walk down the street.

They came to Pete's friend Grumpy Toad, who said, "Come play leapfrog with me! Jumping is easy. Try and see."

Gus jumped and leaped, but he couldn't get over Toad or Pete.

"I wish I could jump like you, but jumping is something I just can't do."

89

Pete said, "Don't be sad, don't be blue. There is something everyone can do!"

On Thursday . . .

Pete and Gus took a walk down the street.

Soon they saw Octopus, who said, "Come juggle with me! Juggling is easy! Try and see!"

"I wish I could juggle like you, but juggling is something I just can't do."

Pete said, "Don't be sad, don't be blue. There is something everyone can do!"

On Friday . . .

Pete and Gus took a walk down the street.

Gus said, "I can't juggle or jump or climb a tree.

It's no fun around here for me."

On Saturday . . .
Pete hoped Gus would come out to play.

"I wish Gus wasn't sad—
I wish Gus wasn't blue—
I wish there was something
we could do."

Just then Pete heard a groovy sound.
It was coming from across the street.
Gus was rocking to his own beat.

SWEET!

Pete said

"Check out Gus the Platypus.
He found something cool he
can do with us!"

TAP

=

THUMP
THUMP

104

GROOVY

The End

**"Be kind whenever possible.
It is always possible."**

—DALAI LAMA XIV

**W**hat a great, sunny morning!
Pete can't wait to play baseball
with his friends.

"Do you want to play catch?"
Pete asks Larry.
  "I can't," says Larry.
"I'm going to the library."

"Do you want to play
catch?" Pete asks Callie.
  "I was about to go for a
bike ride," says Callie.

"Do you want to play catch?" Pete asks John.
"I can't right now," says John. "I have to paint the fence."

Pete wishes his friends would do
what he wants to do. It's no fun
playing catch all by himself.
If only I knew another me . . . ,
Pete thinks. And like that,
Pete has a great idea!

Pete builds a robot! He programs it to be just like him.

"Welcome to the world, Robo-Pete!" Pete says to the robot.
"You're my new best friend. We'll do everything together."

"And I want to play catch," says Pete.
"Great idea!" says Robo-Pete.

Pete and Robo-Pete play catch.

"Wow!" says Pete, running after the ball. "You sure can throw far!"

Robo-Pete throws farther and farther until . . .

"Time out!" says Pete as he tries to catch his breath.
"Let's play something else."
"I want to play whatever you want to play,"
Robo-Pete says proudly.

"How about we play hide-and-seek?" says Pete.
"That will be fun," says Robo-Pete.

Pete finds the best hiding place ever! He's sure Robo-Pete will never find him.

"Ten, nine, eight, seven, six, five, four, three, two, one!" shouts Robo-Pete. "Ready or not, here I come!"

**"Gotcha!"** shouts Robo-Pete, tagging Pete.

"Hey, how did you find me?" says Pete.

"With my homing device," says Robo-Pete.

"I can find anyone, anywhere."

"Okay, enough hide-and-seek," says Pete. "Let's play some guitar."

Pete teaches Robo-Pete how to play a song he made up.

"You have to feel the music,"
Pete explains.
"Okay," says Robo-Pete.

"To feel it, I need to play loud," explains Robo-Pete.

Pete tries to stop Robo-Pete, but Robo-Pete can't hear him over the noise. . . .

"**This is fun,**" says Robo-Pete.

"**This is awful!**" says Pete the Cat.

"Okay," says Robo-Pete. "Let's ride our skateboards instead."

Before Pete can answer, Robo-Pete's feet transform into a motorized skateboard with super speedy wheels.

"Let's go!"

Robo-Pete shouts.

"Wait!" calls Pete.

Pete chases after Robo-Pete. He has no idea where Robo-Pete is going.

Robo-Pete crashes into the sandbox at the playground.
"Are you okay?" Pete asks his robot.

"I am a robot. I am indestructible!" says Robo-Pete.
"What is this strange place?"
"It's a playground," says Pete. He waves to his friends.

"This is Robo-Pete," Pete says to Callie, Larry, and John.
"I made him myself."
"Cool," says Larry.

"We are going to help John finish painting," says
Callie. "And then we are going bike riding."
"I want to go on the slide!" interrupts Robo-Pete.

"Robo-Pete, I want to help my friends paint the fence!"
Pete tells his robot.

"Paint the fence—that would be great," Robo-Pete says. "I am programmed to paint faster than anyone."

Pete and his friends try to help, but Robo-Pete paints too fast.

So instead they ride bikes,

and they read books . . .

and after Robo-Pete is done painting,
they help him clean the brushes.

Pete realizes that it doesn't
matter what they do. Just being
with his friends is what makes it fun!

# The End

**"Opportunity is missed by most people because it comes dressed in overalls and looks like work."**

—THOMAS EDISON

# Pete the Cat

## Construction Destruction

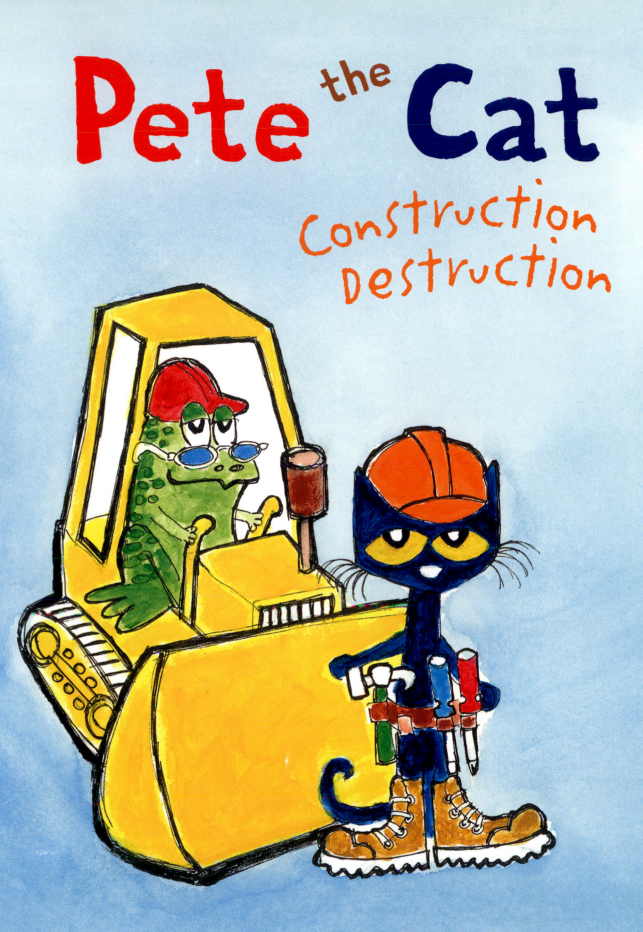

"Recess!" Pete shouts as the bell rings. But when Pete gets outside to play—oh no. The playground is a disaster. The swings are broken, the slide is rusty, and the sandbox is full of weeds.

Pete makes plans for a new playground.

"Wow!" says Principal Nancy. "Can you really build that?"

"Not by myself," says Pete. "I'm going to need some help."

"Whatever you need, Pete, it's yours."

PLANS for NEW PLAYGROUND
By PETE the Cat

The next day, Pete arrives at the playground before school. The construction crew is already there. He gives them the go-ahead to tear down the old playground.

Creak! Crash!

Down goes the slide.

Clink! Clank!

Down go the swings.

**Bang!**
**Boom!** Down goes the tower.

**Honk!**
**Honk!** A truck arrives to recycle the metal.

The new playground equipment has arrived. It's time to get to work. The cement mixer will pour concrete. The dump truck will bring sand and dirt. The backhoe will dig. The whole team will get the job done.

Building a playground is hard work.

The new playground is cool, but it's not cool enough.
"What do you think?" Pete asks, holding up his latest plans.
"It will be too hard to build," says one of the workers.
"And everything is almost finished," says another.

"But it will make this the best playground ever," Pete says.

"Then let's do it," the workers say.

Screwdrivers twist in screws. Wrenches tighten the nuts.

The workers try to make everything perfect.

# Hooray!

The new playground is ready.

Everyone is amazed, until . . .

Creak . . .

creeeak . . .

creeeeeak.

153

Smash! Crunch! Thud!

"Oh no!" says Principal Nancy as the
new playground crashes to the ground.
"The pieces are all mixed up."

Everyone is disappointed—except for Pete.

"It's not how we planned it!" Pete shouts.
"It's even better!"

This playground is filled with surprises and places to explore. The school playground is the most amazing playground ever.

Sometimes you've got to dare to dream big.

# The End

"Be yourself. Everyone else is already taken."

—OSCAR WILDE

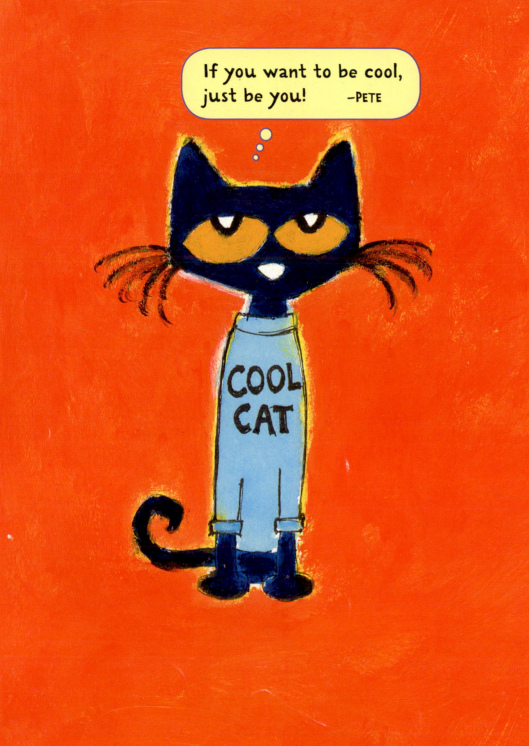